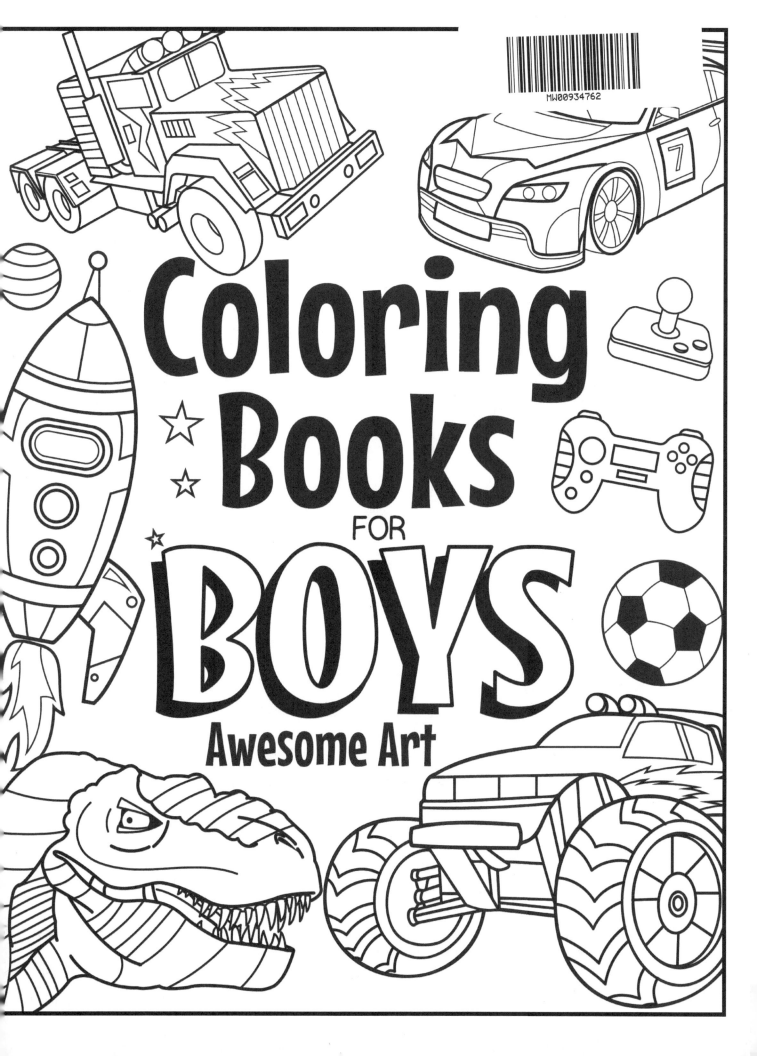

Coloring Books FOR BOYS

Awesome Art

Published in 2024 by The Future Teacher Foundation

© The Future Teacher Foundation 2024

www.thefutureteacherfoundation.com

ISBN: 9798328104340

For printing and manufacturing information please see the last page.

All images copyright © The Future Teacher Foundation 2024

This book contains material previously published in Awesome Coloring Book ages 4-8

If you choose to remove pages for framing, ask an adult to carefully extract with a scalpel and ruler.

Warning: This book is not suitable for children under 36 months of age due to potential small parts - choking hazard.

This book belongs to...

_____

This book belongs to...

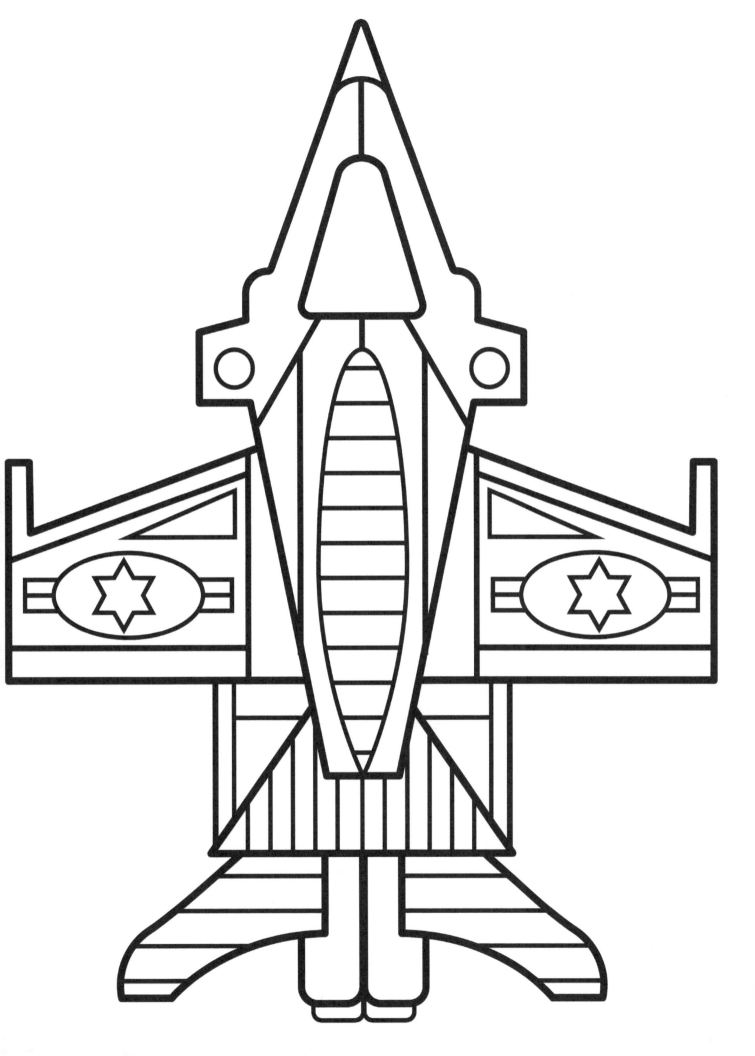

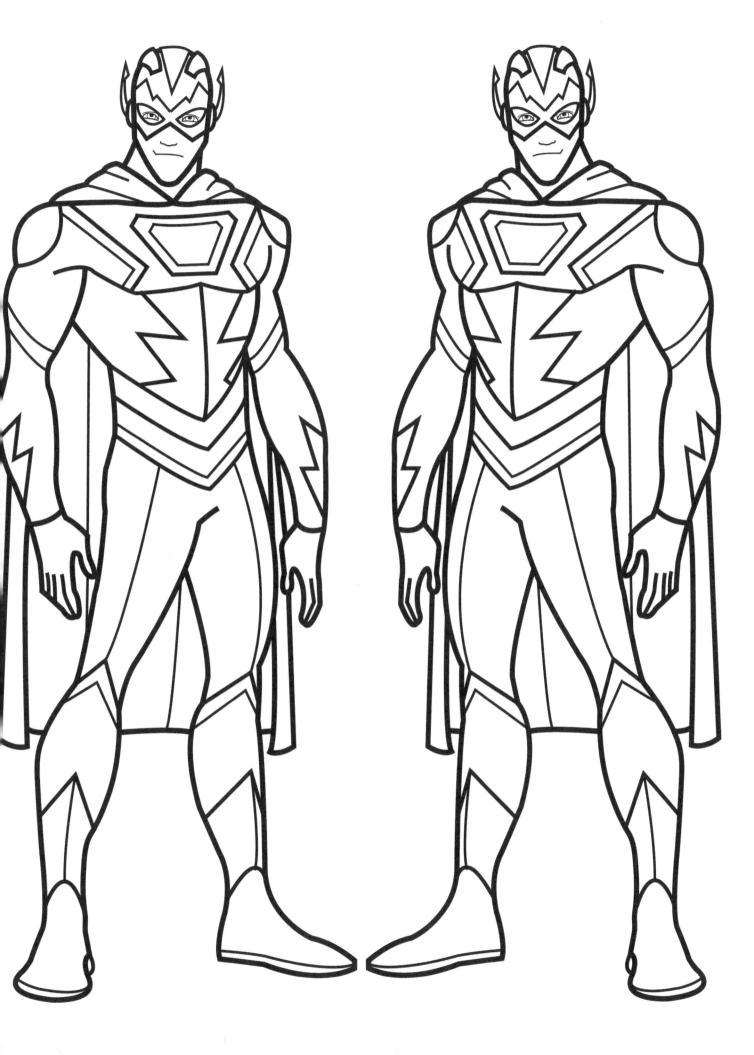

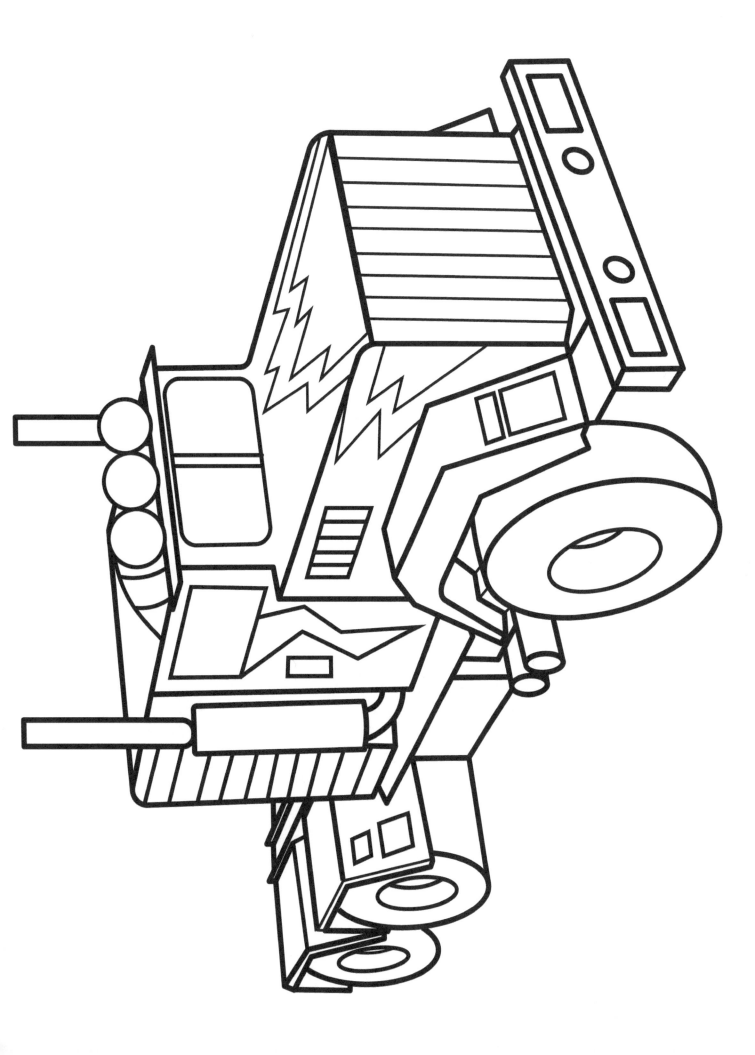

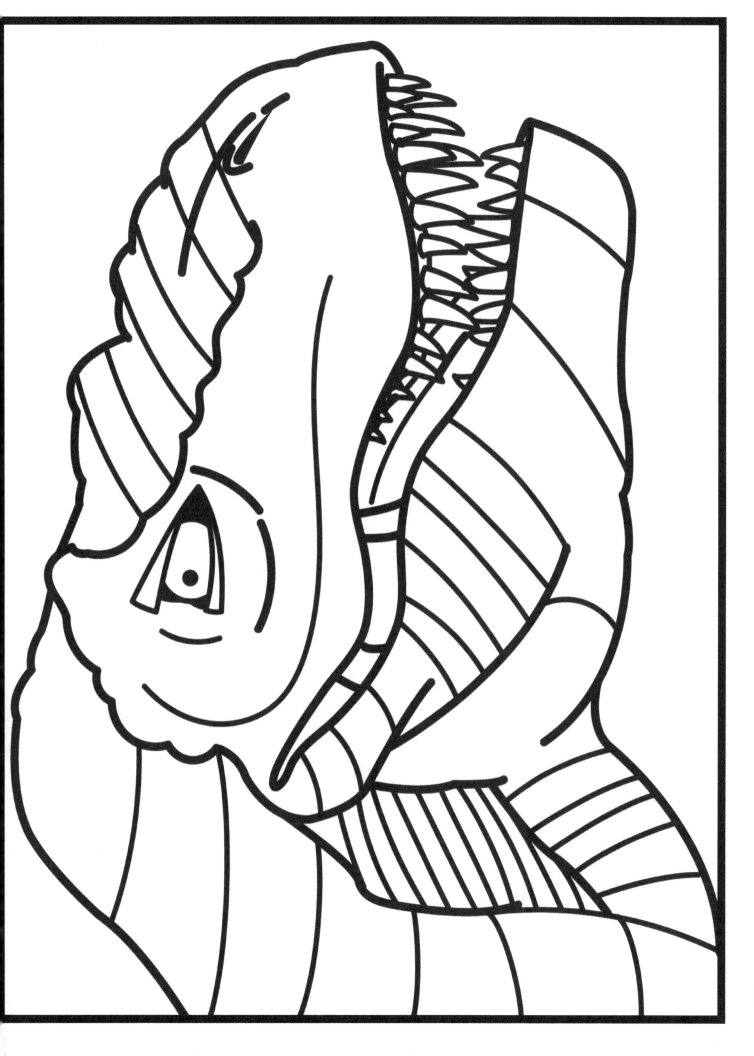

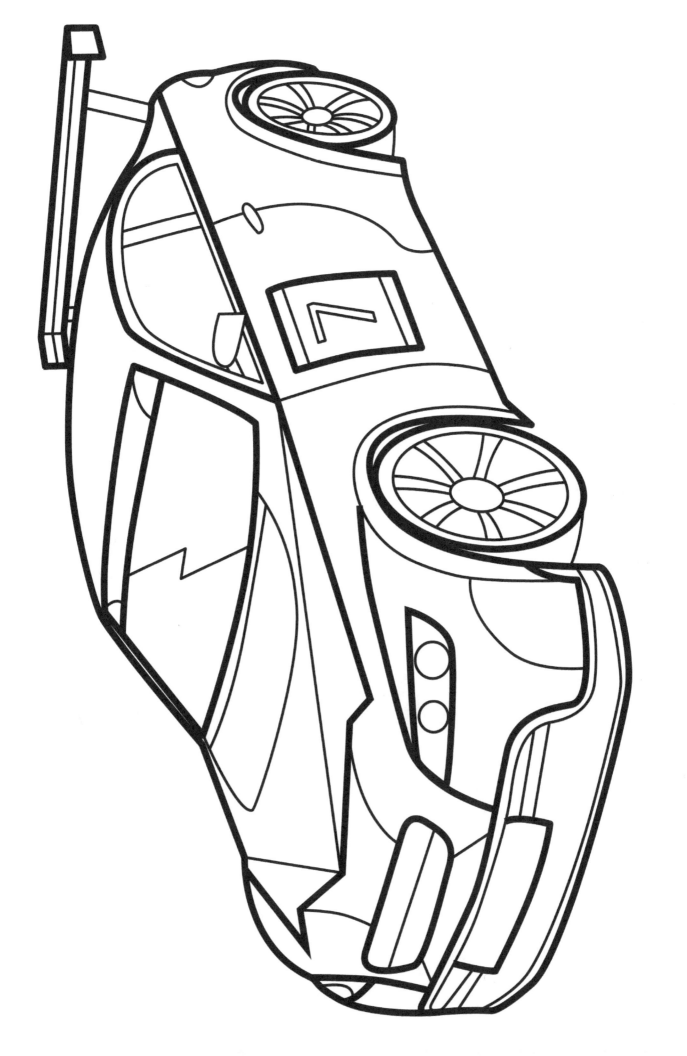

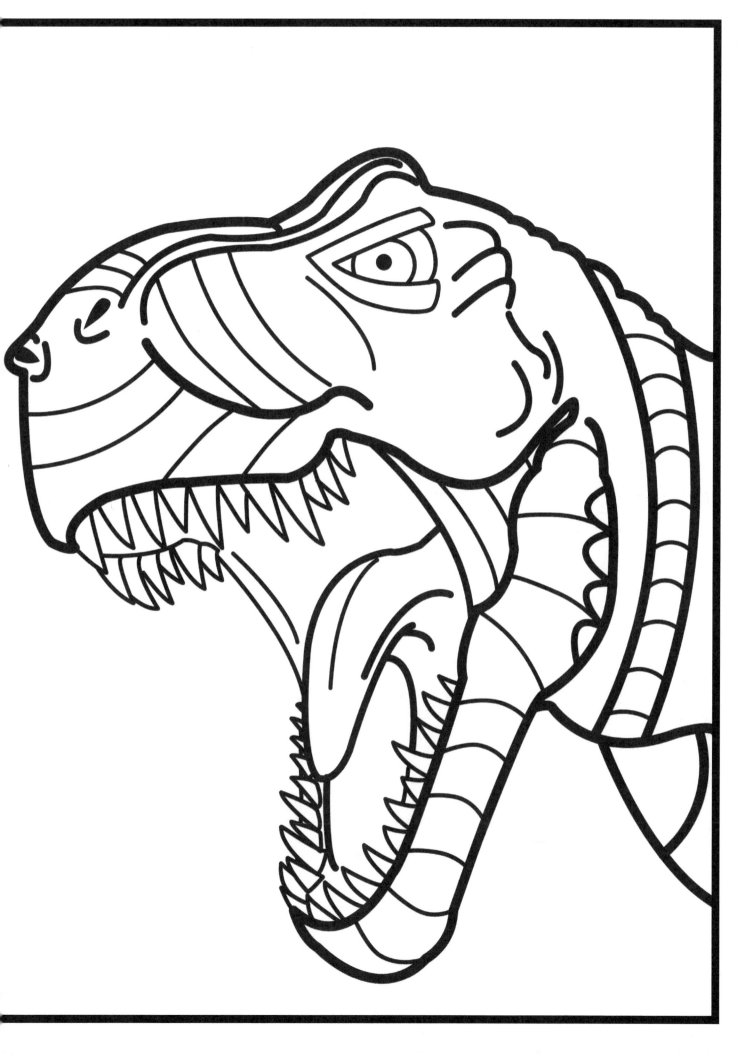

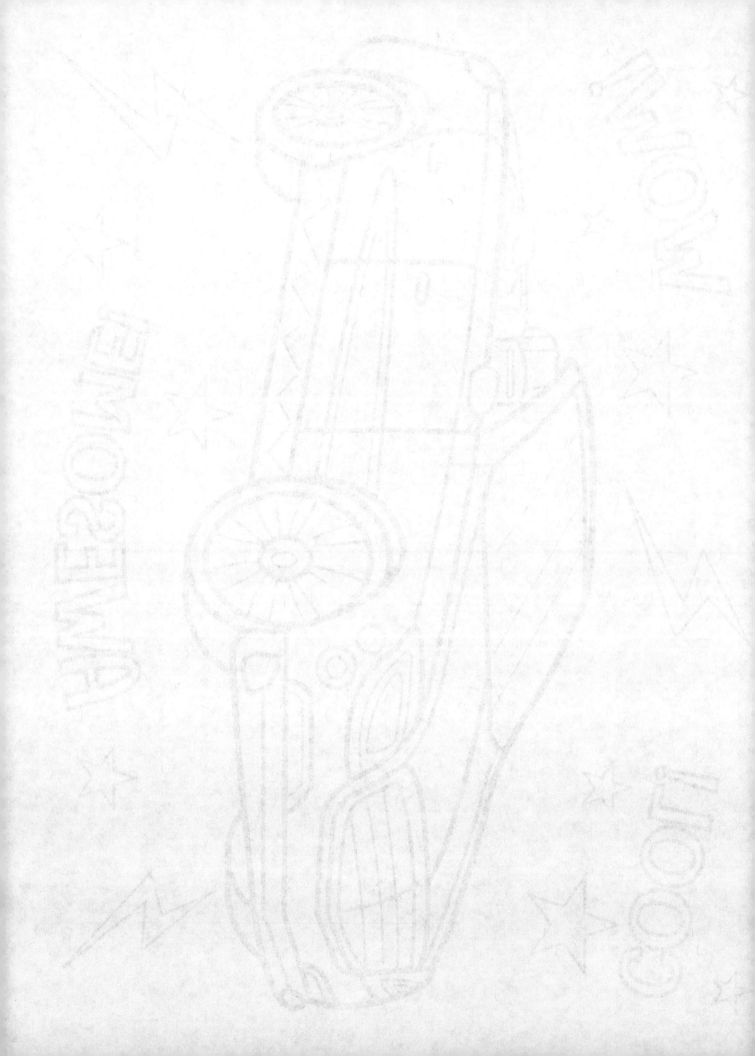

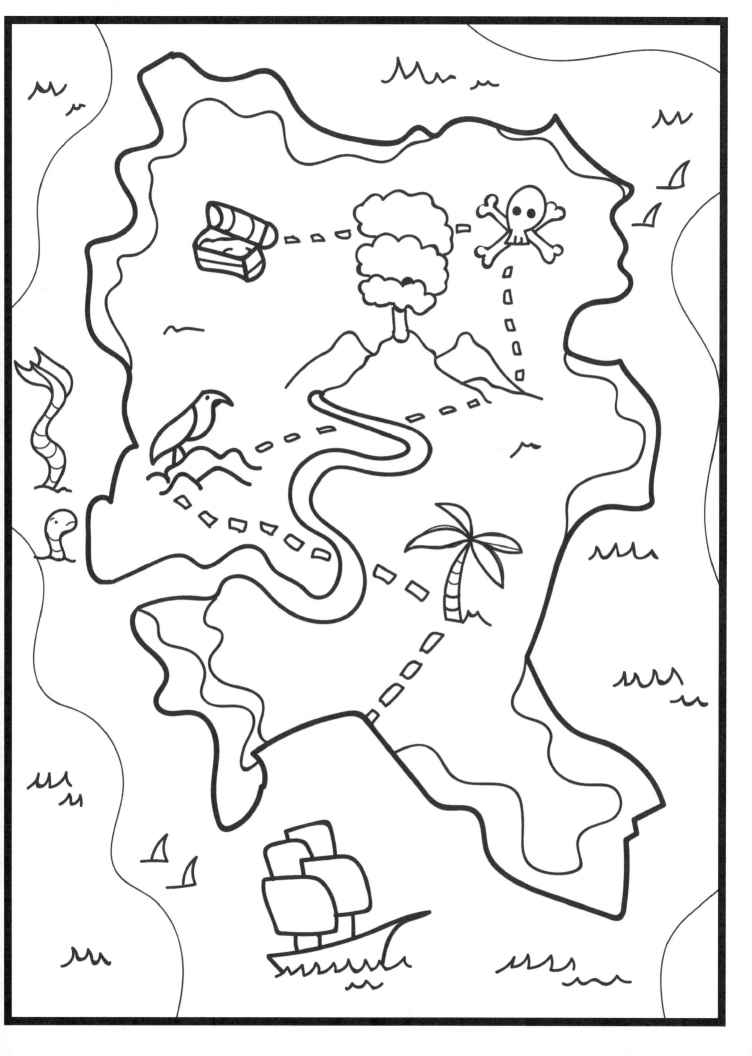

Made in United States
Troutdale, OR
07/10/2024

21134924R00038